PUFFIN BOOKS

The Merman

Dick King-Smith served in the Grenadier Guards during the Second World War, and afterwards spent twenty years as a farmer in Gloucestershire, the county of his birth. Many of his stories are inspired by his farming experiences. Later he taught at a village primary school. His first book, *The Fox Busters*, was published in 1978. Since then he has written a great number of children's books, including *The Sheep-Pig* (winner of the *Guardian* Award and filmed as *Babe*), *Harry's Mad*, *Noah's Brother*, *The Hodgeheg*, *Martin's Mice*, *Ace*, *The Cuckoo Child*, *Harriet's Hare* (winner of the Children's Book Award in 1995) and many others. At the British Book Awards in 1992 he was voted Children's Author of the Year. He is married, with three children and eleven grandchildren, and lives in a seventeenth-century cottage a short crow's-flight from the house where he was born.

Dick King-Smith

THE MERMAN

Illustrated by Frank Rodgers

PUFFIN BOOKS

PUFFIN BOOKS

Published by the Penguin Group
Penguin Books Ltd, 27 Wrights Lane, London W8 5TZ, England
Penguin Putnam Inc., 375 Hudson Street, New York, New York 10014, USA
Penguin Books Australia Ltd, Ringwood, Victoria, Australia
Penguin Books Canada Ltd, 10 Alcorn Avenue, Toronto, Ontario, Canada M4V 3B2
Penguin Books (NZ) Ltd, Cnr Rosedale and Airborne Roads, Albany,
Auckland, New Zealand

Penguin Books Ltd, Registered Offices: Harmondsworth, Middlesex, England

First published by Viking 1997
Published in Puffin Books 1998
5

Text copyright © Fox Busters Ltd, 1997
Illustrations copyright © Frank Rodgers, 1997
All rights reserved

The moral right of the author and illustrator has been asserted

Set in Baskerville

Made and printed in England by Clays Ltd, St Ives plc

British Library Cataloguing in Publication Data
A CIP catalogue record for this book is available from the British Library

ISBN 0-140-38308-5

CONTENTS

CHAPTER 1

MARINUS

Zeta first saw him on the morning of her tenth birthday.

Her present from her mother and father had been a pair of small, but quite powerful binoculars, something she'd wanted for ages, because she was keen on watching birds.

After breakfast in the isolated house they had rented for a holiday in Sutherland, which is about as far north in Scotland as you can go, she had walked down to the beach to watch the gannets diving for fish.

She sat on the low grassy cliff that bordered the long empty strip of pale sand. Elbows on knees, she focused the binoculars on the big white yellow-headed birds as they circled thirty metres above the sea and then plunge-dived, arrowing down to pierce the calm surface, beak first, with a great splash. Judging by the number of birds that were diving, there was a shoal of mackerel not far offshore.

Zeta lowered the binoculars to rest her eyes, and saw, closer in to shore, that several round heads had bobbed up. While she had been watching the gannets, a group of seals had been watching her. She trained the binoculars on them, adjusting the focus so that she could see in close-up each of the sleek, large-eyed whiskery heads as they stared at her with curiosity.

There were five seals, she counted; five heads in a rough circle, and then suddenly another head surfaced in their midst.

For an instant, as Zeta focused on this sixth head, she thought it was another seal that had somehow come up through a bed of seaweed, loose fronds of which seemed to be draped over it.

Then she drew in her breath sharply.

The magnification showed her clearly that the sixth head was not that of a seal but of a man, a man whose long flowing hair lay upon the surface like seaweed.

Like the seals, he was staring at her.

Unlike them, whose faces were expressionless, he was smiling, and soon he raised an arm from the water, first waving it in greeting and then, clearly, beckoning her to come down to the shore.

Zeta's mind was in a whirl. Where could this man have come from? All the time she had been sitting in the August sunshine, watching first the gannets and then the seals, there had been no sign of any bather. Nor would she have expected to see anyone bathing, because there were no other people for miles around. Yet this long-haired head had suddenly popped up.

Should she go down to the beach, as this strange man was indicating? You shouldn't speak to strangers anyway, she knew that. Yet something told her with certainty that there was no danger, and as though in a dream she stood up, replaced the binoculars in their case, slung it round her neck, and began to climb down the shallow cliff on to the beach.

As she walked across the narrow strip of sand –

for the tide was almost at the full – the five seal heads disappeared, and only the sixth head remained.

She could now see that the man's long hair was grey in colour, would be white, she thought, when dry. Yet the face was not that of an old person. It was unlined, the blue eyes were clear, the smile a youthful one.

'What do you want?' said Zeta, standing at the water's edge.

Without answering, the man swam nearer, until she supposed he must have been in his depth, for the upper part of his body rose above the surface. In contrast to the long strands that fell about his shoulders, his brown chest was smooth and hairless. He was slimly built, yet there was a look of strength about him, as you would expect, Zeta thought, of a strong swimmer.

But she could not possibly have expected what happened next. One moment the man was standing, or so it seemed to her, waist-deep. The next, he rose from the waves, leaping as a salmon leaps, and in the instant before he splashed back into the sea, Zeta could see clearly that the lower part of his body was indeed that of a great fish, gleaming, silvery-scaled, tapering to a broad, forked fishtail that slapped the water as he fell

back. Then, with a few powerful strokes of his arms and a swirl of that strong fishtail, he swam right into the shallows, and lay on his side on the white sand in the clear water, chin propped on one hand, his sea-blue eyes smiling up at her.

He's a . . . thought Zeta dazedly . . . no, he can't be, they're always women.

In a shaky voice she said, 'What are you?'

Can he talk? she thought as she spoke. Half man, half fish, will he speak, like one, or be silent, like the other?

The voice that answered was a low and musical one, quiet yet clear.

'I am a merman,' it said.

'But . . .' stammered Zeta. 'But . . .'

'My people are quite like your people in some ways,' said the merman. 'We too have men, women and children as you do. But they are called mermen, mermaids and merbabies. And yes, we can speak, as you now hear. We're rather good singers too. And not bad swimmers, as the seals would tell you.'

'But they can't speak, can they?' said Zeta.

'To you, no. To each other, yes. To me, yes.'

'You can speak seal language then?' asked Zeta.

'I speak all languages – of all the different creatures of the sea, of all the different races of men in the world. I am a very wise old merman.'

One thing's for sure, thought Zeta, you're a bighead.

'I can say this without boasting,' said the merman, seeming once again to be reading her thoughts, 'because it is true. I know almost everything about almost everything. With one exception. I do not know your name.'

'Zeta.'

'Indeed!' said the merman. 'The sixth letter of the Greek alphabet. How strange, Zeta, that your name should be a Greek word, for my name is also in an ancient tongue.'

'What is it?' asked Zeta.

'Marinus,' said the merman. 'Which in Latin means "man of the sea". Tell me, Zeta, how old are you?'

'Ten. Today. It's my birthday.'

I'm surprised you didn't know that, she thought.

'I didn't know that,' said Marinus, smiling. 'We

merpeople can often tell what you humans are thinking or feeling, but we don't know facts about you until we're told. I wish that you may have many happy returns of this day.'

'Thank you,' said Zeta.

I shall certainly never forget it, she said to herself.

'Could you tell me something, please?' she asked.

'Of course.'

'How old are you?'

'Have a guess.'

'You don't look very old. In fact you don't look any older than my dad. Yet your hair is white.'

'What is your father's age?' said the merman.

'Thirty-five.'

'Multiply that by four.'

Frowning, tongue tip sticking out, Zeta struggled with the sum in her mind.

At last, 'A hundred and forty?' she said. 'Are you telling me you're a hundred and forty years old?'

'Round about that,' said Marinus. 'I've rather lost count, to tell you the truth.'

'But that's . . .'

'Impossible? Not for merpeople. We do not age as you do. The sea is a very healthy place to live in, or at least it was when I was young, in the days of sailing ships. But now we face so many dangers, especially pollution. And the world is becoming warmer, it seems. Never before have I swum so far north.'

The merman gave a flirt of his fishtail that sent an extra little wave up the beach, so that Zeta had to jump back.

'Are you not going to bathe today?' Marinus asked. 'The water is very pleasant, and I could introduce you to my friends the seals.'

'I can't swim,' Zeta said.

'I will teach you.'

'No.'

'Why not? You are not frightened, surely?'

'Yes.'

'With me,' said Marinus, 'you will not be. Come down to the beach early tomorrow, while your parents are still sleeping.'

'But . . .' began Zeta.

'No,' said the merman, 'they will not wake until you are safely home again. They will not know, I promise you.'

Then, with a sudden lash of that powerful tail, he swirled back into deeper water and under it and was gone from sight.

Zeta trudged back up the beach and climbed

the low cliff. At the top she turned and took her binoculars from their case. She scanned the mirror-still surface of the grey-green sea.

Far out, a few gannets were still fishing.

Closer in, a couple of seal heads showed.

Of Marinus the merman there was not a sign.

Had she dreamed the whole thing?

CHAPTER 2

THE SWIMMING LESSON

'Binoculars work OK?' asked Zeta's father when she got back.

'Brilliant,' Zeta said.

'See anything out of the ordinary?' her mother asked.

'I saw loads of gannets and some seals,' said Zeta truthfully.

'Fantastic swimmers, seals,' her father said. 'I wish I could swim like they do.'

'I wish you could swim at all,' her mother said. 'If we were ever out in a boat and it capsized or something, I don't know what we should do. You can't swim, I can't swim, and nor can Zeta.'

'What a hopeless pair we are,' said her husband. 'Why neither of us learned as children I can't think. And it's too late now. We'll just have to be content to paddle.'

'Yes, but it's not too late for Zeta,' said his wife. 'And it's no good saying you don't want to, Zeta. You must learn. We can't teach you, obviously, but we must fix something up when we get home again. You have got to have swimming lessons, d'you understand?'

'Yes, Mum,' said Zeta.

In bed that night, she worried about the next day. Would she wake in time, would she be able to slip out without her parents knowing, would Marinus be there waiting? It'd all be all right, he'd said so, but even if it was, would she be able to make herself go in, when she got to the sea?

Throughout the night she kept waking and peering at the luminous hands of the little clock by her bed, until at last, just after five, she saw that it was beginning to get light outside. She put on her swimming costume and over it her dressing-gown, slipped her feet into beach shoes, grabbed a towel, and sneaked out of the house.

Above the beach, Zeta paused a moment, scanning the scene below. There were no gannets fishing, no seals showing their heads, and there was no merman. Only a few gulls floated idly on

the calm sea, while a solitary cormorant flew fast and low across the bay.

Zeta went down to the beach and stood at the water's edge. Perhaps the whole thing had been some sort of weird dream, she thought, or if not, perhaps he's forgotten or just gone away. She felt two conflicting emotions: disappointment that Marinus was not there and relief that he was not, for now she need not go into that cold, scary sea.

She was old enough to know and understand that there were many things of which people were frightened – heights, thunder, spiders, flying. She was frightened of the water.

With a deep sigh that expressed both the disappointment and the relief, she turned away.

'Come on in,' said a voice behind her. 'The water's lovely.' And there was the merman, floating easily upon the surface, his great fishy tail gleaming in the light of the rising sun.

'I don't want to,' Zeta said. 'Please, Marinus, I don't want to, I'm frightened.'

'Of me?'

'No, of the water.'

'Listen to me carefully,' said Marinus. 'If you throw a pebble into the sea, it will sink. But you will not sink, especially in sea water, which is buoyant and holds you up. You will float like a cork. And I will be right beside you and I will teach you how to swim, now, this very morning. With any other instructor, you might need a number of lessons. With me, you will only need one. I promise you that if you trust yourself to me, then in no time at all you will be a swimmer, and more, you will never be scared of the water again.'

How can that be true? thought Zeta. But wouldn't it be wonderful if it were!

'You promise?' she said.

Marinus nodded.

'Leave your things there,' he said. 'The tide is ebbing, they will not get wet.'

As she walked in through the ripples, Zeta was shivering, for the water was cold so early in the day and she was very fearful. Hugging herself, she kept bravely on, knee-deep, waist-deep, chest-deep, while all the time the merman retreated before her. Both his hands were outstretched towards her, but always just beyond her reach, till at last she stood in the calm water up to her neck.

Then Marinus took her hands, and with slow waves of his fishtail swam backwards, pulling her along.

As her feet came up from the sandy bottom,

Zeta knew that now, for the first time ever, she was right out of her depth, and yet, for the first time ever, she was not afraid.

Whether it was the grasp of his strong hands, or his gentle smile, or the look in those sea-blue eyes that were fixed upon hers, she did not know, but whatever it was, she felt relaxed and confident. Even the water seemed suddenly warmer.

'Just beat your legs up and down, Zeta,' said Marinus. 'Keep them straight, don't bend your knees, don't splash.'

Zeta did as she was told.

'Now,' said Marinus, 'I shall let go of one of your hands and you must then use it to pull yourself through the water.'

She did so.

Then without warning he said, 'And the other one too,' and let go of her altogether.

It was too quickly done for Zeta to realize what was actually happening, until Marinus, still close, still totally trustworthy, said softly, 'Zeta, you are swimming.'

'Oh, I am, I am!' cried Zeta. 'Oh, Marinus, it's wonderful!'

Some moments later, the merman said, 'Rest a while now. Let your feet go down till you are upright and then kick down with your legs, first

17

one, then the other, as though you were riding a bicycle.'

Once again Zeta did as she was told, to find that treading water was as easy as pie once you were no longer afraid of it.

'Oh!' she said, turning to look back towards the beach. 'We're a long way out!'

'Do you want to go back?'

'No! No! Not yet.'

'Let us float awhile then. Lie on your back. Spread your arms wide. Just lie upon the water. It will hold you up.'

For a while they lay side by side, rising and

falling gently on the swell, until suddenly Zeta heard a noise near by. A mournful noise it was, as though someone was very sad about something.

She trod water and looked about, and there, all around them, was a ring of seal heads.

'Hoo!' they called. 'Hoo! Hoo!'

'My friends have come to see you,' said Marinus, and he answered, 'Hoo!' in the same plaintive tone.

'They don't sound very happy,' said Zeta.

'But they are,' said the merman. 'They are glad for you, glad that you have conquered your fear, once and for all.'

'I couldn't have done it without you,' said Zeta.

'You couldn't have done it without your own courage,' said Marinus. 'And now you must swim back to shore. You must be home in plenty of time, before your parents wake.'

'Goodbye!' cried Zeta to the seals, and she turned and swam towards the beach.

Grabbing her dressing-gown, shoes and towel, she scrambled up the sandy cliffs and turned to look back.

The seals were gone, the bay was empty and still, until suddenly, far out, a great fishtail came up out of the water and slapped down again upon the surface with a loud triumphant thwack.

Back at the house Zeta hid her wet swimming costume. They mustn't know, she thought. I'll dry it later somehow.

She felt terribly happy and, suddenly, rather tired and sleepy. She put on her pyjamas and got back into bed.

The next thing she knew, an hour or so later, was that her mother had drawn back the curtains and was standing by her bed.

'Come on, sleepyhead,' she said. 'Breakfast's nearly ready,' and she bent to stroke Zeta's head.

'Funny,' she said. 'Your hair feels damp.' She laughed. 'Just as though you'd sneaked out of the

house and gone down to the beach for a bathe.'

'Oh, honestly, Mummy!' said Zeta. 'How could you imagine that? You know I can't swim.'

CHAPTER 3

THE MESSAGE

'Hurry up and get dressed then,' Zeta's mother said. 'I forgot to tell you – the fish-man came yesterday.'

Zeta shot up in bed.

'What!' she cried.

'The fish-man. You know, he comes once a week from Durness in his little van. I bought some fresh mackerel. I know you like them.'

It might have been all right if only the fish hadn't still looked so lifelike after cooking. A glance at the tail of the one on her plate, an exact miniature of the merman's, and Zeta knew she could not possibly eat it.

'I don't want mine,' she said.

'Whatever's the matter with you?' her mother

said. 'You love mackerel.'

'I just don't feel like it,' Zeta said.

'I'll have it,' said her father. 'I can eat two, no problem.'

'You're not ill, are you?' her mother said.

'No, I'm fine,' said Zeta, and she ate two extra pieces of toast and honey to show that she was.

'What shall we do this morning?' said her father once breakfast was finished and the washing-up done. 'I feel pretty sharp – must be eating all that fish. Good for the brains, they say. Let's do something interesting and exciting.'

'You've come to the wrong place,' his wife said. 'There's nothing specially interesting or exciting in this remote bit of Sutherland.'

'Oh yes there is!' said Zeta.

'Such as?'

Zeta had spoken without thinking, but now she thought fast. For the merest fraction of a second she was tempted to tell them about meeting Marinus. But they'd never believe her. Anyway,

she didn't want them to know. It was a secret, between her and the merman.

'Oh, like the gannets and all the other birds we never see at home, like the guillemots and the razorbills and the puffins.'

'You and your birds,' her father said. 'You're a proper twitcher, you are.'

'Well, you never know, Dad,' said Zeta. 'I might see something really rare today, now that I've got my binoculars.'

Like a merman, she thought, but I shan't tell you if I do.

'Let's all go for a long walk,' said her mother. 'Right around the bay to the far end. We can do a bit of beachcombing on the way.'

'There won't have been anything much washed ashore,' her husband said, 'what with neap tides and calm weather. A few jellyfish and some mermaids' purses, that'll be about all.'

'Are they really the purses of mermaids, Dad?' Zeta asked.

'No, of course not, they're just the empty egg-cases of the skate or the ray. I thought you'd have known that. There aren't really such creatures as mermaids, Zeta. Except in fairy tales.'

As they walked along the beach, Zeta kept looking seawards through her binoculars. There must have been a big shoal of fish far out in the bay, for as well as the diving gannets a school of porpoises was hunting.

At first Zeta could not think what she was looking at, as the black barrel shapes rolled up and under in their switchback pursuit of the fish, but then she realized.

'Look!' she cried. 'Porpoises!' and she took one hand away from the binoculars to point.

Even as she did so, she saw to her dismay that the little whales had been joined by another shape, a brown-backed, silvery-tailed, long-haired shape that swam beside them, surfacing as they surfaced, diving when they dived.

'There's something funny out there!' her father said suddenly. 'Lend me your glasses, Zee, will you please?'

Oh no! thought Zeta.

'Quick!' her father said. 'They'll be out of sight round the headland before long.'

Zeta handed him the binoculars, hoping against hope that Marinus would somehow, with his strange gift of foresight, know what was happening and would dive from sight.

'Odd!' her father said after a little while. 'I thought for an instant that I saw a man amongst those porpoises. Hard to see at that distance with the naked eye, specially with the sun glinting on the water, but I thought I saw a man's arms, as though someone was swimming with them.'

'Can I look?' his wife said, and then, 'No, nothing there but porpoises.' And then, 'They're gone now,' and she handed back the binoculars to Zeta.

'I didn't know porpoises came this far north,' her father said.

'It's because the seas are getting warmer,' Zeta said.

'Really? Who told you that?'

'A teacher,' said Zeta truthfully. For Marinus has already taught me to swim, she said to herself, and who knows what else he may teach me? He said he knew almost everything about almost everything.

They walked on, but, as Zeta's father had said, it didn't look like a good beachcombing day. There were a few bits of driftwood that would have been worth collecting had it been wintertime, and they saw a pair of hooded crows picking over something very dead. Otherwise, the long strip of white sand was empty of interest.

But on their way back from the far end of the beach, Zeta saw a small object some way ahead that seemed to be rolling in and out in the ripples.

She turned the binoculars on it and then saw what it was.

'A bottle!' she cried. 'Perhaps it's got a message in it, from a shipwrecked sailor, cast away on an island somewhere!' and she ran on ahead.

'A message!' her father said. 'Oh, to be ten years old again and let imagination run riot.'

But then they saw Zeta racing back.

'Look!' she shouted. 'I was right!' And there, inside the bottle she carried, was a piece of paper.

'What fun!' her mother said. 'Get it out and see if there's anything written on it, Zee.'

Zeta uncorked the bottle and turned it up, but shaking would not get the paper out, so she ran up to the high-tide mark and found a thin stick. Probing with this, she managed to draw out the scroll of paper. When she smoothed it out, she could see that there was indeed writing on it, printing that read

Alexander Jarvie
Stuart Street, Durness
Finest fresh fish
delivered weekly
to your door

'It's a sheet of the paper that the fish-man wraps his fish in!' said her mother. 'However did it get into that bottle?'

'Perhaps Mr Jarvie is cast away somewhere,' said her husband.

Zeta felt disappointed. To find a bottle with a scroll of paper in it but no message except the address of the fish-man was an awful let-down.

But then, as she held the paper up to the sunlight, she saw that there was writing on the other side of it.

'Oh, look!' she said.

They looked and saw, in big black capitals

NUMBER SIX. SAME TIME TOMORROW
M

'Whatever can that mean?' said her mother.

'Someone called M wants Mr Jarvie to deliver six fish at the same time tomorrow, I suppose,' said Zeta's father. 'Though Heaven knows when tomorrow was. That bottle might have been floating about for ages. It seems a funny way to order your fish, whoever M may be.'

But Zeta suddenly knew who M was and who Number Six was.

'The sixth letter of the Greek alphabet.' She

31

could hear the quiet musical voice. Zeta.

The message had indeed come from another, quite different, fish-man.

What would tomorrow bring?

CHAPTER 4

THE COWRIE
NECKLACE

That night Zeta did not keep waking to look at the clock. She was so confident of the merman's powers – magical powers, she now knew – that she told herself he would fix it for her to wake early, and for her to return without her parents knowing.

By half-past five next morning she was on the beach, waiting. There was no sign of Marinus, but then a seal popped its head up right in front of her.

'Hoo! Hoo!' it moaned, and began to swim along towards a group of flattish rocks that stuck out into the sea. It wanted her to follow, Zeta saw, because it kept looking back at her and calling.

When she reached the rocks, she climbed over

them and there, lying on the largest, flattest one, was the merman.

Seeing him out of the water for the first time, Zeta realized what a wonderfully strange figure he was.

Above the waist, half of a handsome man, lying propped up on one elbow, his long hair – dry now – as white as snow.

Below, half of a beautiful fish, the long tail drooping over the edge of the rock so that its flukes just touched the surface of the water.

In the sea, this lower half had appeared silvery before, but now Zeta could see all the many different hues of the scales, glinting in the early morning sunlight; silver, yes, but as well there were blues and greens, in fact all the colours of the rainbow, it seemed.

To the waiting seal Marinus called, 'Hoo-hoo!' in a brisker, less sad tone, which meant, Zeta guessed, 'Thank you!' and the animal dived from sight.

'Good morning, Marinus,' Zeta said. 'I got your message. But I've been thinking – how could

you have written it? Where could you have got a pen, and one with such very black ink? And how did you find that paper?'

'Mr Jarvie must have dropped it, I suppose,' said Marinus. 'Perhaps when he was delivering your mackerel . . .'

'However did you . . .?' interrupted Zeta, and then, 'Sorry. Go on.'

'. . . and probably the wind blew it about, and perhaps a bird picked it up and carried it for a while. At all events it finished up on this rock, and then when I saw an empty bottle bobbing about in the water, I simply couldn't resist sending you a message. I thought you'd enjoy it. So after I'd had my swim with the porpoises, I dropped the bottle close inshore, while you were all at the far end of the beach.'

'How did you know . . .?' began Zeta again, and again she checked herself. *He just knows these things,* she thought.

'I still don't see how you wrote the message,' she said.

'Easy,' said Marinus. 'I borrowed some ink from a passing cuttlefish and wrote with the quill of a herring gull's wing-feather. I shan't need to bother again, because you will come every morning now, won't you?'

'Oh yes! Oh, but we've only got ten days of our holiday left, Marinus, and then we go home, all the way to the South of England. And we don't live anywhere near the sea, either. I shall never see you again.'

'You may come back to Sutherland another year, surely?'

'Oh yes, I hope so. But how will you know?'

'I shall know. Now then, we have but ten days, and there's a lot for me to teach you.'

Zeta frowned, thinking of her classroom in her school, picturing her teacher writing sums on the blackboard, seeing herself watching a programme for schools on the television or reading in the library, surrounded by books on every subject, and by atlases and dictionaries and encyclopedias. How could Marinus teach her anything, here on a rock by the sea?

He smiled.

'I have no blackboard, no books,' he said, 'but I have gifts that no other teacher has. Anything that I show you how to do, you will never forget.'

'Like swimming?'

'Like swimming. And today we will go under the water as well as on it. I will teach you how to hold your breath and how to dive beneath the waves like the porpoises and how to open your eyes under water and see the wonder of the creatures that live there. But as well as telling you what to do, I can tell you a number of things about the world, and because you hear them from me, you will always remember them. Do you believe me, Zeta?'

'I believe you, Marinus.'

'Good. Now before we swim this morning, I am going to tell you something, a piece of general knowledge if you like, just to show you what I mean. Listen. A planet is a heavenly body that moves around a star. The major planets, in order from the sun, are Mercury, Venus, Earth, Mars,

Jupiter, Saturn, Uranus, Neptune and Pluto. Now, let us swim.'

Following Marinus as he swam out into the bay, Zeta kept saying to herself, I simply cannot understand how I was ever scared of the water. What wonderful stuff it is. It carries me so that I feel as light as air. And without waiting to be told, she took a deep breath and put her head under and opened her eyes, to see a swarm of little fish flashing away before her.

By the end of that morning's bathe, Marinus had taught her how to swim on her back, how to porpoise-dive, and, at the end of the lesson, how

to dive from the flat rock into the deep water below it. Within minutes she was diving like an Olympic champion.

Marinus looked at the height and position of the sun.

'Time you were getting back,' he said.

'Where shall we meet tomorrow, Marinus?' Zeta asked as she prepared to leave.

'Here, on this rock,' said the merman.

That afternoon they drove the dozen miles into Durness to do some shopping. Zeta, sitting in the back of the car, suddenly noticed a sign that said STUART STREET, and then, halfway along, a shop with a notice above its window:

ALEXANDER JARVIE
FISHMONGER

Her thoughts jumped to the other fish-man. Or man-fish, was he?

She looked at her watch. Fifteen hours till she would see Marinus again. I'd like to buy something for him, she thought, but what could I possibly get? He has no house to keep things in, no pocket to put things in. A watch to go on his wrist? But she hadn't enough money, because it would certainly have to be an expensive water-proof one. And anyway, she thought, I bet he can tell the time exactly, by the sun or the moon or something, wherever he is, in the seas off Northern Scotland, in the Mediterranean, under the toe of Africa, amongst Australian reefs or Caribbean islands. Because of course he can travel anywhere he likes in the oceans of the world. Perhaps I shall see something in the shops that he might like.

'Dad,' she said, 'I haven't had any pocket money since we came on holiday.'

'Nor you have, Zee,' he said, and when they had parked the car, he gave her four pound coins.

'Bit extra,' he said, 'just in case you see some-thing you specially fancy.'

And, in a knick-knack shop, she did.

It was a necklace made of cowries; each glossy, pinky-brown little shell held together by a length of thin twine threaded through its inrolled lip.

When she asked if she might try it on, and undid its catch and clasped it around her neck, it was plenty long enough, she felt certain, to go around the neck of a man. Most men might not have liked to wear such a thing, but she was sure that the merman would. And it cost exactly four pounds. She bought it.

When, the following morning, they met again
on the flat rock, Zeta took the necklace from her
dressing-gown pocket and held it out.

'I bought this for you, Marinus,' she said, 'to
remind you of me.'

The merman took it gently from her, looked at
it, smiling, and fastened it around his neck. It
fitted perfectly, an elegant little collar round the
brown throat.

'I thank you, Zeta,' he said. 'I shall always wear
these beáutiful tiny gastropods.'

'They're cowries,' said Zeta.

'They belong to a class of molluscs that include

snails and limpets and sea hares. The term gastropod comes from two Greek words, one meaning
stomach, one meaning foot. A lovely present from
a girl with a Greek name. By the way, Zeta, what
is a planet?'

'A heavenly body that moves around a star,'
replied Zeta.

'Name the major planets.'

'In order from the sun?'

'No. The other way round. Start with the one
that's furthest away.'

'Pluto,' said Zeta, 'Neptune, Uranus, Saturn,
Jupiter, Mars, Earth, Venus and Mercury.'

CHAPTER 5

THE BASKING SHARKS

'Pluto,' said Marinus, 'takes two hundred and forty-eight Earth years to orbit the sun.'

'Who was Pluto, anyway?' asked Zeta.

'The Greek god of the dead. Each of the planets is named after a Greek or a Roman god, or goddess in the case of Venus.'

'Except Earth.'

'Yes, it's always seemed strange to us merpeople that this planet is called Earth.'

'Why?'

'Because it is seventy per cent water.'

'Tell me some more things, Marinus,' Zeta said.

'What about your swimming?'

'Not this morning. I don't need to, I know how.

Let's just sit here and you teach me about the world.'

So Marinus told her first about the continents and how, over many millions of years, the land masses had moved and changed their shapes, pushing and shoving against one another, so that new seas and lakes were formed and new mountain ranges were thrown up. These movements were still going on, he said, though very, very slowly.

Then he spoke of the sea itself and of the creatures that live in it, from the great whales to the tiny plankton – microscopic animals and plants that float and drift on the oceans, providing food for many of those whales and many fish.

And lastly he talked of the heavens that are above land and sea, about the galaxy of the Milky Way with its hundred thousand million stars. In particular he spoke about the Moon, the satellite of the Earth, that orbits it every 27.32 days.

'It is the force of gravity between the Earth and the Moon,' he said, 'that causes the tides, pulling the water of the seas twice – first one way, then the other – every twenty-four hours and five minutes.' Everything that he told her stuck for ever in Zeta's head. She would never forget, not because she was a specially gifted child, but because all these facts and pieces of information came from the lips of Marinus the merman.

Later that day the weather changed as a belt of rain swept across from the west. Zeta was reading a book. Her mother was writing postcards. Her father was doing a crossword.

'"Flat-footed mollusc",' he said to his wife. 'Nine letters beginning with G and ending in D.'

'Haven't a clue,' she said.

'Gastropod,' said Zeta.

'What?'

'Gastropod, Daddy. It comes from two Greek words, meaning stomach and foot.'

'How in the world did you know that?'

'It's something I learned at school,' said Zeta. Which is true, really, she thought. Marinus is my new teacher and already I've learned an awful lot.

Her father wrote in the answer.

'Well, thanks, Zee,' he said. 'Perhaps you can help me with another one I'm stuck on. Because of your gastropod, I now know it begins with a P, but I can't make any sense of the clue. Listen. '"Microscopic, not a piece of wood with a weight on it".'

'Plankton,' said Zeta. 'Get it? Plank . . . ton.'

Her father raised his eyebrows in amazement.

'Perhaps we'd better swap,' he said. 'You finish the crossword, I'll read your book. What is it, anyway?'

'It's an old encyclopedia that I found in the bookshelves,' Zeta said.

'Oh, so that's where you're getting all this new-found knowledge, is it?'

Zeta smiled.

The book lay open at the M's, and she read:

Mermaid a legendary creature whose form is that of a beautiful woman above the waist and a fish below. A mermaid's male counterpart is called a merman.

Legendary indeed! she said to herself. I wonder what he'll teach me about tomorrow?

The next morning she was woken even earlier than usual by a tapping at her window. She drew back the curtains and there, sitting on the sill, was a gull, staring in with cold yellow eyes.

'Kee-ow!' it cried, and flew off in the direction of the sea, only to return again and again, calling all the while, as though to say, Zeta thought, 'Follow me!'

Remembering the seal of two days ago, Zeta hastened to obey.

The gull flew, not to the flat rock, but towards the part of the beach where Zeta had found the bottle, and there she saw Marinus waiting, a little way offshore.

'Kak-kak!' he cried to the gull in thanks, and, waving to her, cried, 'Hurry, or we'll be too late.'

Zeta left dressing-gown and towel and shoes above the high-water mark and ran into the grey-green water in her blue swimming costume.

'Too late for what?' she called. 'What about lessons? Aren't you going to tell me things, like yesterday?'

'I'm going to show you things,' Marinus said. 'Very exciting things. We must hurry or they may be gone. They're round the next headland, out in the deep water channel, too far for you to swim on your own and, anyway, you wouldn't be fast enough. Climb on my back and put your arms round my neck.' And, when she did so, 'Hold

tight!' he said, and, with a swirl of that great fishtail, they were off.

What a ride that was. Before, the merman had always swum slowly with her, at her pace. Now he went at top speed, far faster than any man could have swum, tail lashing just beneath the surface, arms pulling just above, the water creaming past them as they shot across the bay and rounded the point.

'What is it?' cried Zeta as they sped along. 'What is it that you're going to show me?'

'Some big fish,' said Marinus.

'What sort of big fish?'

'Sharks.'

'*Sharks!*' cried Zeta. 'Here?'

'Yes, three of them.'

'But – but, Marinus,' gasped Zeta. 'They may attack us!'

'They will not, Zeta,' said the merman. 'They are basking sharks. They are plankton-feeders. They only eat those tiny creatures, but, I warn you, they themselves are very big. Let us just hope they have not moved on elsewhere. It was around here that I met and spoke with them an hour ago, and I sent the nearest gull to fetch you.'

Suddenly he stopped.

'I can feel the vibration of them,' he said. 'They

are close. Slip off my back and tread water, while I dive.'

'We are lucky,' he said when he rose again. 'They are near the surface. They will pass very near, just beneath us. Take a deep breath and look below.'

If her face had not been under water, Zeta would have gasped with amazement at what she saw.

Coming slowly towards them was the most enormous fish, its huge mouth stretched wide as though propped open – wide enough, Zeta could see, to swallow a cow whole. But this mouth was entirely filled with a sieve-like plate (called baleen, Marinus told her later), through which only micro-scopic creatures could pass.

Very slowly, paying them no attention at all, the basking shark swam past them, followed, Zeta could see as she took repeated breaths of air and submerged again, by two others equally as huge.

Each fish, she learned later from the merman, was over twelve metres long and weighed around ten tonnes.

In line ahead, the squadron of basking sharks moved below them in stately silence, until, with a slap of his tail upon the surface, which meant, Zeta supposed, 'Goodbye,' the merman no longer

followed, but lay in the deep water beside her, smiling.

'Are they not magnificent?' he said.

'Wonderful!' said Zeta. 'I only hope that people don't hunt them.'

'Not nowadays,' said Marinus. 'They used to hunt them, long ago.'

'For food?'

'Yes, but mostly for their livers. One third of each basking shark is its liver, and from that the people of these coasts and islands used to make oil, to light their lamps in the long winter.'

Clinging to the merman once more as they sped home, Zeta said, 'Before long it will be winter. Where will you go, Marinus?'

'South, like the swallows,' he said. 'To blue waters and hot sunshine.'

'But you will come back here next year?'

'Only if you do.'

CHAPTER 6

THE BOAT TRIP

Each early morning now followed the same routine. Zeta would meet Marinus on the flat rock, they would have a swim, and then back to the rock for lessons.

They didn't feel a bit like lessons to Zeta though, for the merman taught her so many interesting things on so many different subjects, chopping and changing about through English and Maths and History and Geography and Science.

'You had better have a smattering of a foreign language too,' he said. 'Probably French will be the most useful to you.'

So he taught her enough of French vocabulary and grammar 'so that you can make yourself clearly understood in France'.

There was no need, of course, to test her on any of this new knowledge. Once in her head, it was there for good, they both knew.

'Oh, Marinus,' said Zeta one day. 'If only I could just stay here with you, I wouldn't ever need to go to school again. They wouldn't be able to teach me anything more.'

'They will,' said Marinus. 'There's no end to knowledge, it's growing all the time. I've not had long enough to tell you a tiny fraction of the things you might like to know.'

'It feels like an awful lot to me,' said Zeta. 'My teacher at school will be amazed.'

'I'd go easy on that if I were you,' said the

merman. 'It doesn't pay to be too much of a clever clogs, people don't like it.'

'But I could be top of the class.'

'You will be, but just be modest about it. Don't act the know-all. It's all right to help with the odd couple of clues when your father's doing his crossword, but don't go solving the lot for him.'

'However –' began Zeta, and then of course stopped. 'But supposing we do go to France one day,' she said. 'Mum and Dad are bound to wonder how I can speak the language.'

'Don't you do French in your class at school?'

'Yes, a bit.'

'Well, you learned it very quickly.'

'But what about me swimming? They still think I'm like them and can't swim a stroke.'

'True,' said Marinus. 'We'll have to arrange to do something about that.'

'What?'

'Wait and see.'

At breakfast that morning, Zeta's father said to his wife, 'D'you realize that we're coming towards the end of this seaside holiday and we've never yet been on the sea?'

'In a boat, you mean? Well, I suppose it's partly because we're all non-swimmers. Like I've said before, I'm always a bit afraid a boat might capsize or something.'

'In this lovely calm weather we've been having? Anyway, I wasn't thinking of handling a boat ourselves – we could hire a boatman to take us all round the different islands and inlets. It'd be nice for you, Zee, there'd be masses of birds to see, and seals too.'

But not a merman, thought Zeta. She knew now that he would never show himself to anyone but her.

'Do you know of a local boatman who could take us?' asked Zeta's mother.

At that precise moment they saw a van pass the

window and stop outside the house. It was Mr Jarvie the fish-man, on his weekly visit.

'No, but he might,' said Zeta's father.

And, of course, he did.

'Is it fishing you were after?' said Mr Jarvie when they asked him. He looked a little worried at the thought that these people might want to catch their own fish rather than buy his.

'No, no,' said Zeta's parents. 'We shall want to buy some of yours now. No, we just want to go on a boat trip.'

'Is it sailing you want?'

'No, no,' they said. A sailing boat's more likely to capsize, each thought.

'Is it today you want to go out?' said the fish-man.

'Yes,' they said. 'Yes, why not? It's a lovely day.'

'You have come to the right man,' said Mr Jarvie. 'My cousin, Peter Mackay, has a grand motor boat and he has no one booked for today. I know, for he told me so, not an hour ago. I'm away back to my shop in Durness this moment. Call in there as soon as you like and I'll direct you to him.'

'Can he swim?' asked Zeta's mother.

'Peter? Aye, he can swim,' said the fish-man. 'Why?'

'Oh, nothing.'

Zeta's father looked at his watch.

'We'll be at your shop in an hour's time, Mr Jarvie,' he said. 'If you'll be good enough to warn your cousin.'

Somehow it came as no surprise to Zeta to find that Peter Mackay's boat was called *Mermaid*. What's Marinus up to? she thought.

She had brought her binoculars of course, and how grateful for them she was, because as well as the many kinds of seabirds that she expected to encounter, there was a lovely surprise for her.

As the boat entered a distant cove, the greatest bird of those parts came soaring out from the land as though purposely to greet her.

'Kya!' cried the golden eagle in its high yelping voice, as it glided and swung in wide circles high above the boat, before beating away inland again.

There was time for each of them to take a turn with the binoculars, and it was while her father was focusing them upon the great bird and her mother and the boatman were looking up at it too, that Zeta, watching some distant seals, suddenly thought she saw a strange head bob up amongst them, as had happened at her first sight of Marinus.

She stood up in the boat, the better to see, at the same moment as her father turned to her to hand back the binoculars, the eagle having gone from sight.

All at the same time, his elbow caught her in the side, she caught her foot in a coil of rope in the well of the boat, and the *Mermaid* heeled over a little as Peter Mackay altered course to round a headland.

Over the side and under the water she went.

'She can't swim!' shouted her mother and father to the boatman, and Zeta's father began to fumble with the lifebelt that hung on the boat's side.

Peter Mackay cut his engine.

'Dinna throw yon lifebelt, sir,' he said quietly. 'She can swim, no doubt of that.'

And as they stared in open-mouthed amazement, they could see how right he was.

As soon as she hit the water, Zeta realized this

was all Marinus's doing. He had fixed it so that they would now know. But what am I to say? she thought as she struck out back towards the boat.

Yet even as she thought it, she knew that somehow the merman would put the right words in her mouth.

'Sit tight, lady and gentleman,' said Peter Mackay as the swimmer approached. 'Leave it to me to pull the lassie aboard.'

Once he had done so, Zeta's parents said exactly the same thing in exactly the same tone of voice at exactly the same moment.

'You swam!' they cried.

Zeta sat on the thwart before them in her soaking wet clothes, happily dripping.

'I did, didn't I?' she said.

'But how? You were always so scared of the water, and look at you now, grinning all over your face as though you'd enjoyed it.'

'I did,' said Zeta. 'It's easy, really.'

'But how did you learn?'

'Well,' said Zeta truthfully, 'someone once told me that all you have to do is to beat your legs up and down, keeping them straight, and pull with your arms. So that's what I did. It's like if a kitten or a puppy falls in the water, I suppose. It just swims, automatically.'

'Are ye telling me,' said Peter Mackay as he started up his engine, 'that this lassie has never in her life swum before?'

'Never!' they said.

'Swimming like a fish!' the boatman muttered in wonder, shaking his head. 'A mermaid aboard the *Mermaid*!'

CHAPTER 7

THE SEAL PUP

'You were watching yesterday, weren't you?' said Zeta to Marinus when she reached the flat rock the following morning. 'You fixed it for me to fall overboard, didn't you?'

'What an idea,' said Marinus. 'Are you angry with me?'

'No, of course not,' said Zeta. 'Oh, the look on their faces! They still can't believe that somehow I just swam instinctively.'

'They have to believe it though, don't they?' said the merman. 'They have no choice.'

'I'm going to make them come down to the beach and watch me swimming, later on this morning,' said Zeta. 'In case they thought it was all a dream.'

'Good girl,' said Marinus. 'You're as brave as the lion under whose sign you were born.'

'Leo, you mean?'

'Yes, July 23rd to August 22nd. We met on your birthday, August 9th.'

'What sign were you born under, Marinus?'

'Pisces, of course. February 19th to March 20th. And just to be different, I was a leap year merbaby. February 29th 1856. So I only get a birthday every four years. Shall I teach you a rhyme about the twelve signs of the zodiac?'

'Please.'

> 'Our vernal signs the RAM begins,
> Then comes the BULL, in May the TWINS;
> The CRAB in June, next LEO shines,
> And VIRGO ends the northern signs.
> The BALANCE brings autumnal fruits,
> The SCORPION stings, the ARCHER shoots;
> December's GOAT brings wintry blast,
> AQUARIUS rain, the FISH comes last.'

'Just think,' said Zeta. 'You've lived about fourteen times as long as me. I wonder how long I shall live?'

'D'you want me to tell you?' said Marinus.

'You know?'

'Not precisely. There are limits to the powers

with which I am blessed. But I can tell you roughly. Give me your hands, palms up.'

For a while the merman stared, first at Zeta's left hand, then her right. Then he smiled at her.

'Lucky old you,' he said.

'Why?'

'You are going to have a long and happy life. You have a great many more birthdays to look forward to. And, talking of birthdays, come now and swim with me, and I will show you someone who was born this morning, not an hour ago.'

'What? Who?'

'Wait and see,' said Marinus.

Together they swam along, not far offshore, till they came to another rocky outcrop, in the face of which was a cave.

Marinus hauled himself out of the water and Zeta followed.

From inside the cave came an angry growl, which ceased as the merman made soft reassuring noises in reply.

'Don't stand up,' said Marinus. 'She will think it a threat. Wriggle forward on your stomach, as I have to.'

At the lip of the cave Zeta peered in. Once her eyes became accustomed to the gloom, she could see, lying within, a grey seal. Why has he brought me here just to see an old seal? she thought. But then the animal moved a little, to show, lying by her side, a newborn pup.

'A baby!' breathed Zeta. 'But it's white!'

'They are born white and woolly,' said Marinus. 'It will shed that coat when it's six weeks old or so, and grow another, yellow dappled with grey. For the next three weeks it will just lie here and get very fat indeed on its mother's rich milk.'

'Won't it go in the sea?' Zeta asked.

'It would drown if it did. The pups of the common seal can swim straightaway, but these are grey Atlantic seals. That baby won't take to the water till next April.'

'Is it a boy or a girl?' said Zeta.

'I'll ask,' said Marinus, and he made some cooing noises to which the mother seal replied with a soft sighing sound.

'A boy,' said Marinus. 'You're very lucky to have seen him, he's the first to be born around here. Grey seals don't usually pup till early September. Come on, we'll leave them in peace.'

'Just think what I've seen on this holiday!' said Zeta as they swam back. 'As well as the gannets and all the other seabirds, I've seen a golden eagle and three basking sharks and a newborn seal pup!'

'And an old merman,' said Marinus.

Who looks so young, thought Zeta, apart from his white hair.

'How much longer d'you suppose you will live, Marinus?' she said.

'None of us knows, do we?' said Marinus. 'Man or woman, merman or mermaid, we cannot tell. Some, very ill or very old, may know that they are close to death, but most wake one morning, never dreaming that that day will be their last on Earth. Or, in my case, in the sea.'

When they had hauled themselves out on to the flat rock, Zeta said, 'But you will know, won't you, Marinus? When it's your last day, I mean. You know everything.'

'Almost everything,' said the merman. 'Not that. Now then, this is a gloomy sort of conversation to have on a fine sunny morning. Let's talk of something else. What would you like me to tell you about?'

'Tell me what was happening in the world when you were a little merboy. Was there television?'

'Oh, heavens, no!' said Marinus. 'That wasn't invented till 1926, when I was seventy.'

'So there wasn't radio either?'

'Not till 1895.'

'No telephones?'

'Not till 1875.'

'What about cameras?'

'Yes, there were cameras. The first photograph was taken in 1826, thirty years before I was born.'

'I wish someone had taken a picture of you when you were a merbaby,' said Zeta.

'No one has ever photographed me. No one has ever seen me, in all my long life, except you. You are the only human to whom I have ever shown myself.'

'Why me?'

'You happened to be in the right place at the right time,' said Marinus. 'More, you are of the right age. Children like you, imaginative, sensitive children, can accept matters of magic and mystery in a way that no older person could. It is because of your age that you will always remember the things that I have told you, even when you are a very old lady, talking with your great-grandchildren.'

'Will I tell them about you?'

'I cannot know that, but you will know, when the time comes, if there is one who will believe you. Tell him, or her. Now then, it's time for you to go.'

'Oh, Marinus!' said Zeta. 'Tomorrow morning we're going home. When you and I meet here early, it will be for the last time.'

'Will it?' said the merman.

'The last time this year, I mean. Oh, I wish we weren't going.'

'I shall go too, Zeta,' said Marinus. 'The year is drawing on and the water growing colder. I too shall go south, but a good deal further south than you. Run home now, before your parents wake.'

Later that morning, Zeta's mother and father stood together on the beach and watched their daughter run into the water and swim like a seal.

'I have never heard of such a thing,' said Zeta's father to his wife. 'A child that has always been scared of the water suddenly learning to swim, all on her own, and swim so well too. I simply can't believe it.'

'We have to believe it though, don't we?' said his wife. 'We have no choice.'

'Wonderful!' they cried when Zeta came running out of the sea. 'If only we could swim like that too.'

Zeta grinned, remembering what her mother had once said.

'We must fix something up when we get home,' she told them. 'You have got to have swimming lessons, d'you understand?'

'I'm too old to learn,' her father said.

'Oh, come on, Dad,' said Zeta. 'I know someone who's four times as old as you and he's a brilliant swimmer.'

Her father laughed.

'You may know about gastropods and plankton,' he said, 'but your arithmetic's not much good. Someone four times my age would be one hundred and forty years old!'

CHAPTER 8

THE PARTING

That afternoon, their last, they decided to go for another trip in Peter Mackay's boat. This time they went in the opposite direction, heading south along the coast, cruising along not far from the shore.

At the end of their own long strip of beach the boatman brought the *Mermaid* in quite close to the flat rock.

There was of course no merman to be seen on it, but a little further along Zeta noticed some big cork floats bobbing on the surface, and Peter Mackay cut his engine beside one of them and began to haul in the line attached below it.

'Please,' said Zeta. 'What are you doing?'

'Catching lobsters, I hope, missy,' said the boatman, but when the wickerwork lobster pot came to the surface, it was empty. So were the rest.

'No luck then,' said Zeta's father.

'It's a strange thing,' said Peter Mackay. 'This is the very best spot for lobsters on this coast, yet these last weeks I've not taken a single one.'

'Perhaps they escaped from the pots?' said Zeta.

'They canna do that. Once they get in through the hole in the top, they haven't the brains to go back out the same way.'

'Perhaps someone helped them,' said Zeta.

'Helped them?'

'Told them how to get out.'

'Don't be silly, Zee,' her father said.

They went on as far as the next outcrop of rock, where the seal's cave was. There's a fat white baby in there, thought Zeta, but none of you knows that, just as none of you knows who saved the lobster's lives, but I bet I do.

As usual, there were masses of birds for Zeta to train her binoculars on, and there was an extra treat in store for her. By great good luck she saw a little flock of very small seabirds, blackish, with white rumps and squared black tails, fly past them in the strangest manner.

They flitted along just above the waves, their

black feet dangling so that they appeared to be running on the water.

'Oh, look, Mr Mackay!' cried Zeta. 'What are those?'

'Those are storm petrels,' said the boatman. 'Some folk call them Mother Carey's chickens. You're lucky to see them, they're usually much further out at sea.'

I've been lucky in so many ways on this holiday, thought Zeta. But now it's nearly ended. By this time tomorrow we'll be well on our way home. If only Marinus could come with us.

She grinned to herself, imagining Marinus sitting beside her on the back seat, the seat belt across his brown chest and across his middle, where flesh met scales, his great tail somehow

curled around and tucked between them. Talk about a fish out of water!

'Mr Mackay,' she said as they approached the quayside at the end of their trip, 'why did you name your boat *Mermaid*?'

'She's bonnie to look at and she is mistress of the seas, as mermaids are.'

'But surely you don't believe there are such creatures?'

Peter Mackay, standing braced at the wheel in the little cockpit, looked at her for a moment without answering.

Then he said, 'Do you believe in them?'

'Oh yes!' said Zeta, and her parents laughed.

'She's got quite an imagination,' her father said.

The *Mermaid* glided in to the quayside steps and they all alighted.

'I'll be honest with you, missy,' said Peter Mackay, and he slapped the gunwale of his boat with a large horny hand. 'The only mermaid I've ever set eyes on is this one.'

'Early bed for you tonight,' her mother said that evening. 'We've got to be off at the crack of dawn.'

'Oh no!' cried Zeta.

'What's the matter? It won't hurt you to get up

a bit early for once in a while, Zee. Daddy wants to get the bigger part of the drive over with tomorrow.'

'What time have we got to get up?'

'I'm setting my alarm for five o'clock,' said her father. 'Mum and I will be going to bed early too.'

I shan't see Marinus, Zeta thought wildly. There won't be time. Oh, what shall I do?

For a while she lay sleepless, but when at last she did drop off, there came a series of strange dreams.

In one, she went into Mr Jarvie's fish shop in Durness, and there, behind the counter, was a large lobster, wearing a striped apron and serving customers with fish that he held in his huge claws.

In another, she was in the seal's cave, and the mother seal said to her, 'Do you not think my son is beautiful?'

'Yes,' she replied. 'What is his name?'

'Beau,' said the seal.

'Beau?' said Zeta. 'But that is French for beautiful.'

'Exactly,' said the seal.

It was a third dream, however, that woke her. She was sitting on the flat rock beside Marinus, and he said to her, 'What happens every 27.32 days?'

'The Moon completes an orbit of the Earth,' said Zeta.

'Exactly,' said Marinus. 'And tonight the Moon is very bright.'

Zeta jumped out of bed and drew back the curtains. Outside it was almost as bright as day, though her watch told her it was only just after midnight.

Very quietly, she dressed and tiptoed downstairs, and then, once clear of the house, ran like a stag for the beach. She scrambled down the low cliff, raced along the sands to the rocky outcrop, and climbed on to the flat rock.

There was the merman, sitting with his fishtail hanging over the edge, his long white hair falling about his shoulders, the cowrie necklace around his throat glinting in the moonlight.

'Marinus!' she panted. 'I mustn't stay long, they might wake and find my bed empty, but I had to come now because we're leaving early and Dad's set his alarm for five o'clock.'

'I know,' said Marinus. 'Anyway, long drawn out goodbyes are not a good idea. Better to clasp hands in friendship and part.'

'But only till next year?'

'I told you – if you come here then, so shall I.'

'Where are you going now?'

'To the Mediterranean, I think, to the South of France. The Côte d'Azure should still be pleasant at this time.'

He held out his hand and Zeta took it.

'I can't stop, I must hurry back,' she said. 'And thank you, thank you for all that you have done for me.'

She climbed off the rock and began to run along the beach, stopping once to turn and call back to him.

'*Au revoir*, Marinus!' she cried. '*Au revoir!*' but by then she was too far away to hear him say, 'Adieu.'

CHAPTER 9

THE FRENCH HOLIDAY

It was broad daylight by the time they had packed the car. The road that led from the house ran along the top of the low cliff that backed the beach, and Zeta, gazing seawards as they left, could see the gannets already diving for fish. The flat rock was bare.

I wonder if my teacher has already gone, she said to herself.

She thought of the other teacher, in whose classroom she would soon be sitting again, and remembered how Marinus had warned her against being a clever clogs.

It won't be easy, she thought, because I know so much more than I did at the end of last term, so many things that the other children won't know.

It wasn't easy, either, she found when term started. There were so many questions to which she knew the answers when no one else did, and she had to keep firm control of her right arm to stop it shooting up in the air when the teacher asked the class something. Not always, of course, because sometimes a subject would come up where she couldn't resist showing off her new-found knowledge.

They chanced to be doing an animal project for the first few weeks, and the class teacher was most impressed (and somewhat surprised) at Zeta's familiarity with the ways of such creatures as seals and basking sharks and storm petrels.

Zeta was not surprised though when the next project turned out to be 'The Universe'. Marinus fixed it somehow, she thought, as she rattled off the answers to questions about the planets and about the effect of the Moon on the movements of the sea.

One day her teacher kept her back after school.

'Zeta,' she said, 'I want to tell you how pleased with you I am. You seem to have picked up a great deal of knowledge since last term. How have you managed it? Where did you get all these bits of information from?'

'From an encyclopedia,' said Zeta.

An encyclopedia, she knew, contains information about almost everything, so Marinus was one, wasn't he?

But it was in French lessons that she really let herself rip. Because of the crash course that the merman had given her, she now had a head start on even the cleverest of the other children, and learning more of the language was, she found, a great pleasure.

During the term, Zeta's teacher had mentioned to her parents how well she was doing, but even so, they were very surprised at her end-of-term report. Before, Zeta's reports had been quite satisfactory – she was an average child, it seemed, whose work was adequate but unremarkable – but now they read:

Zeta has come on by leaps and bounds, in all subjects. She has really blossomed this term, having acquired, it seems, a great deal of general knowledge. She has become especially fluent in French, in which subject she has completely outstripped the rest of the class.

'It's amazing!' her parents said to each other. 'First, she somehow teaches herself to swim, and now, it seems, she's practically educating herself!'

'What's all this about your French?' they asked

her. 'How have you picked it up so quickly?'

'I suppose it's a bit like the swimming,' Zeta said. 'I just suddenly found I could do it. I like it, it's fun. I wish we could go to France one day.'

Many months later, she remembered this remark.

It was the middle of the summer term, so that her eleventh birthday was not far away, and, thinking of this and remembering her tenth, she said, 'What date is it that we're going to Sutherland this year?'

Her parents looked at each other.

'We didn't tell you before,' her mother said, 'because we thought it would be a lovely surprise, but we're not going to Scotland this year.'

'Not going!' cried Zeta.

'No,' said her father. 'We've booked a holiday in France, just like you wanted.'

Both of them looked so pleased that Zeta tried her hardest to hide her disappointment. Now she wouldn't see Marinus! He'd be waiting on the flat rock . . . oh no, he wouldn't, come to think of it. She remembered him saying, 'If you come here, then I shall.' So now he wouldn't swim north. But perhaps he might still be on the Côte d'Azure?

'Whereabouts in France?' she asked. 'Is it by the sea?'

'No, it's quite a way inland, in the Dordogne. You don't sound too pleased.'

'Oh, I am,' Zeta forced herself to say, 'but please, can we go back to Sutherland next year? I did so love it there.'

'All right,' they said.

'To the same place, to the same house?'

'If it isn't already booked by then.'

'You could book it now, a year ahead. Please!'

'All right,' they said.

In fact, once she got over her disappointment, Zeta much enjoyed their holiday in France. Her French, she soon found, was a great deal better than her father's or her mother's, and she chattered away happily to everyone she met.

'You are English, mam'selle?' asked a shop-keeper.

'Yes.'

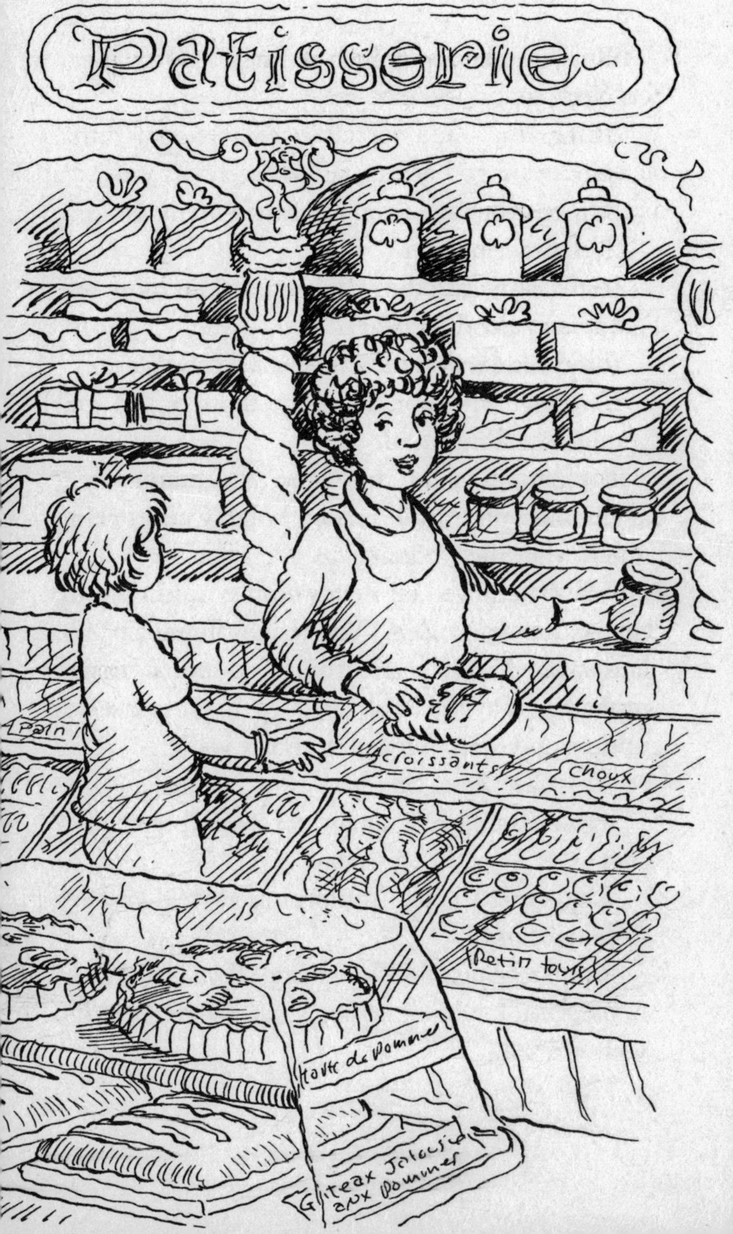
Patisserie
Pain
croissants
Choux

'But you 'ave zee French mother?'

'No.'

'Father?'

'No.'

'Ah, but you 'ave been to France many times?'

'No, never before.'

'*Formidable*!' said the shopkeeper. 'You must 'ave 'ad a vairy good *instituteur*.'

'I did have a good teacher,' said Zeta.

I wonder what you'd say, she thought, if I told you he was a merman.

Back home again, they were all sitting, looking at photographs of the French holiday and talking about what they'd done.

'I really enjoyed it,' Zeta's mother said. 'Mostly thanks to you, Zee. You're so fluent in the language that it made things so much easier, instead of having to struggle to make ourselves understood. You enjoyed it, didn't you?'

'Yes,' said Zeta. She had.

'How about going again next year?' her father said.

'Dad!' cried Zeta. 'You promised we'd go back to Sutherland!'

'Only teasing,' her father said. 'I've booked the house. You'll be able to see your old gannets and your old seals.'

And my old merman, thought Zeta. But not for another whole year. I'll be twelve and I'll have grown a lot, and he'll be a hundred and forty-two and look exactly the same, just as young, apart from his white hair.

'I can't wait,' she said.

'The time will fly,' they said.

CHAPTER 10

THALASSA

The time did fly. Always before, it had seemed to Zeta that the holidays sped past while the terms dragged slowly by.

But now things were different. Ever since she had met Marinus, she had somehow found her schoolwork much more interesting. To the delight of her parents and her new teachers, she continued to shine (no one was surprised when she won a special prize for French) and to enjoy her work. So that the first three terms at her secondary school seemed to go like lightning.

In no time at all they were once more setting out for Sutherland. This year Zeta's parents had planned a more leisurely journey, stopping two nights on the way. So the final leg of the drive was a short one, and they arrived at the holiday house not long after midday.

As soon as she could, Zeta took her binoculars and went down to sit on the sandy cliff.

Seal heads popped up to stare at her, but no other head surfaced amongst them as it had two years ago.

Still, he must know I'm here again, she thought; he said he'd come if I did. And tomorrow I'll wake early, I'm sure of that.

At five the next morning she woke feeling terribly excited. In a few minutes, ten minutes at most, she told herself, I shall see my merman once again.

Something put her off the idea of bathing – there'd be too much to talk about when they met on the flat rock – so she dressed in jersey and jeans and slipped out of the house.

When she reached the low cliff, she heard, to her surprise, the sound of someone singing. A girl's voice it was, high and pure and clear, singing a wordless song, like a bird's trill. It seemed to be coming from the rocky outcrop.

Zeta scrambled down the cliff and ran along the beach and began to climb up. The singing had stopped, and there was no sound but the shrill 'Kleep-kleep!' of a flock of oystercatchers further along the beach.

As she came in sight of the flat rock, Zeta's mouth was open, ready to call, 'Marinus! It's me!' But then she closed it.

There was indeed a figure waiting there – a figure with long golden hair, so long that it fell to the rock – sitting facing away from her, looking out to sea.

Zeta felt both disappointment and anger. She was disappointed not to have found Marinus there, at their special meeting place, and angry that this person, this holidaymaker, the singer, she supposed, should have chosen to sit there. Which was, presumably, why the merman had not shown himself. Wherever had the wretched girl come from?

Before she could speak, the intruder began to sing once more, but this time the song had words:

'We are the folk of the circling seas,
Grey seas, green seas, seas as blue as the sky.
On the ocean's roll we take our ease
As the swell dips low, as the swell swings high.
In storm or calm, we go as we please,
Singing our song as the waves run by.
We are the fishtailed folk of the seas,
Grey seas, green seas, seas as blue as the sky.'

Zeta, listening, suddenly saw that this was no human holidaymaker.

'Oh!' she gasped as the song ended. 'You are a mermaid!'

'And you,' came the reply, 'are Zeta.'

Going forward, Zeta could see the fishtail hanging over the lip of the flat rock. She could see the face now, a young and lovely face that broke into a slow smile.

'Sit by me,' said the mermaid, patting the rock.

'How do you know my name?' Zeta said.

'My grandfather told me.'

'Your grandfather? You are Marinus's grand-daughter?'

'I am.'

'What is your name?'

'Thalassa,' said the mermaid.

'Is that a Greek word, like mine?' asked Zeta.

'Yes. It's the Greek word for "sea".'

You're so young, thought Zeta, you can't be more than seventeen. How could a merman of a hundred and forty-two years old have a grand-daughter your age?

As though she knew what Zeta was thinking, Thalassa said, 'I'm not as young as you might think. I have already lived for what you humans consider a reasonable time – three score years and ten. We do not age as you do, as no doubt Marinus told you.'

'But where is he?' said Zeta. 'Two years ago he said he would come back here if I did. And then last year I couldn't because we went to France. But why is he not here now?'

The mermaid stretched out a hand and took hold of Zeta's.

'Zeta,' said Thalassa, 'we merpeople live long, long lives, but we do not live for ever.'

'Oh,' said Zeta softly. 'What are you trying to tell me?'

'That my grandfather is dead. He died, peacefully, some months ago. But before then he told me about you, Zeta, and asked me to come here to meet you.'

'Why did he die?' said Zeta miserably.

Thalassa smiled, squeezing her hand gently.

'He was very, very old, you know,' she said. 'A hundred and forty-two years is not a bad age. When you and he met two years ago, he sensed that he had not much time left.'

'Oh, Thalassa,' said Zeta. 'I can't believe that I'll never see Marinus again.'

'You will always remember my grandfather,' said the mermaid. 'All through your long life, for he told me that you will live to be a very old lady.

He also said that some day, when you are talking with one of your great-grandchildren, you may tell that child about the merpeople. Lastly, he wished you to have two gifts, one of which you have already had.'

'What was that?'

'The words and the music of the song that you have just heard me singing, as he told me to. Should you yourself sing it beside the sea, here or anywhere in the world, and there are merpeople within hearing, they will come to you.'

Zeta could not speak, for her heart was so full – of sadness, yes, but of joy too, to think that though Marinus was no more, Thalassa was here in his place, and that there would be others, some day, somewhere.

At last she found her voice.

'Did you say there were two gifts?' she asked.

For answer, Thalassa threw back her long mane of golden hair and reached up to unfasten what was around her throat: the necklace of cowries.

'Grandfather valued this above everything,' she said, 'because it was a present from you, Zeta. "Give it back to her," he told me, "with my love."'

Carefully the mermaid clipped it around Zeta's neck.

Then she slid off the flat rock into deep water.

She surfaced once to wave a slender arm, and then she dived with a great smack of her fishtail upon the surface, that sent up a fountain of water-drops, golden in the light of the rising sun.

CHAPTER 11

LONG AFTERWARDS

A lifetime later, in the year 2066, two figures sat side by side on that same flat rock by that same beach in Sutherland, by now one of the few unspoilt places in the British Isles.

One was an old lady of eighty.

One was a small boy aged five.

The old lady's name was Zeta, but the child, who was her great-grandson, called her by the pet name that all her many descendants used.

'Grannyzee,' he said, 'do you believe in mermaids?'

'Of course,' said his great-grandmother. 'Mermaids and mermen and merchildren and merbabies. What made you ask?'

'Mummy read me a story about them. I wish I

could see one.'

'Shall I sing you a song about them?' asked the old lady.

'Yes, please,' said the boy.

So the old lady sang:

'We are the folk of the circling seas,
Grey seas, green seas, seas as blue as the sky.
On the ocean's roll we take our ease
As the swell dips low, as the swell swings high.
In storm or calm, we go as we please,
Singing our song as the waves run by.
We are the fishtailed folk of the seas,
Grey seas, green seas, seas as blue as the sky.'

As the last notes died away, suddenly there was a swirl in the water below the flat rock.

'Oh, look, Grannyzee!' cried the small boy. 'Just look!'